# 1

THE campers had gone. Slyly and silently they had stolen away in the night.

They had arrived in September and taken possession of the bit of flat ground near the pond. It was thought that they came from the west country, but no one knew anything about them for certain. They were what rural folk called *diddakois* – people who led a wandering life but were not true gipsies.

Their caravan was towed by a shabby old car. For additional accommodation they pitched a tent alongside it. The two boys slept in the tent. The little girl slept in the caravan with her parents.

The man appeared to have neither craft nor trade but to rely on casual work. He had been taken on at Halsey's farm up the road, and it was by Mr Halsey's permission that he occupied the site near the pond. For it was a time when extra help was welcome. After harvest and threshing were over he was put to digging a drainage ditch across one of the pastures. This took him until the end of November, for the land was heavy and he was single-handed. When it was done the farmer paid him off. There was no other casual work to be had in the neighbourhood so after a few days the family moved on. Their going caused little comment and no regret. The woman was slatternly and her children were not encouraged to play with those of the cottage people.

It was at Halsey's farm that the man had found the striped kitten. It was one of a population of cats that lived in the yards and sheds and granaries, and it was about three months old when the man picked it up and asked if he could take it home to his children. Permission was readily given. There were too many cats about the place.

The kitten took gladly to its new life, which was a big improvement on the precarious existence from which it had come. The campers were kind to it and entertained by its antics. It was much fondled and amply fed. In the bright autumn days it played around the camp, chased leaves and followed the children when they gathered mushrooms or late blackberries. In the evenings it sat under the table while the family were at supper and at night it slept in the bunk bed beside the little girl. As the days

PUFFIN BOOKS
*Editor: Kaye Webb*

# THE SNOW KITTEN

'They seemed so fond of it,' remarked Mrs Mostyn to Mrs Reece. 'Whatever come over them to leave it behind?'

'Too mean to feed it, I dare say,' said Mrs Reece, staring over the pond at the dishevelled campsite where Mr Halsey's temporary farm worker had lived in his caravan until he disappeared one night, leaving an unpaid bill for eggs and vegetables, a pile of empty tins, and his children's playful tabby kitten with the white feet.

The kitten was a pretty little thing, but no one wanted it. Mrs Mostyn's old dog wouldn't put up with it, Mrs Reece had too many mouths to feed, and the Trims wouldn't have it because of the unpaid bill. The only person who could give it a home was Miss Coker, and she was sour as vinegar to everyone and had a particular hatred of cats. 'No use asking her,' said all the grown-ups.

So as winter advanced the snow kitten got thinner and weaker and colder while the gulls ate the meagre food put out for it, and the marauding fox drove it out of its only shelter. But the children remembered it and tried to work a miracle in time for Christmas.

It's a common enough event, a cat being abandoned, but Nina Warner Hooke makes us see the kitten's loneliness and hunger as if it were the very first time it had ever happened.

# THE
# SNOW KITTEN

NINA WARNER HOOKE

*Illustrated by Gavin Rowe*

PUFFIN BOOKS

Puffin Books, Penguin Books Ltd, Harmondsworth, Middlesex, England
Penguin Books, 625 Madison Avenue, New York, New York 10022, U.S.A.
Penguin Books Australia Ltd, Ringwood, Victoria, Australia
Penguin Books Canada Ltd, 2801 John Street, Markham, Ontario, Canada L3R 1B4
Penguin Books (N.Z.) Ltd, 182–190 Wairau Road, Auckland 10, New Zealand

—

First published in Puffin Books 1978

—

Copyright © Nina Warner Hooke, 1978
Illustrations copyright © Gavin Rowe, 1978
All rights reserved

—

Made and printed in Great Britain by
Richard Clay (The Chaucer Press) Ltd,
Bungay, Suffolk
Set in Linotype Pilgrim

shortened it spent less time outdoors and more in the caravan, discovering the delicious luxury of warmth. With the lamp lit and the paraffin stove hissing under the cooking pots the caravan was a cosy place. The harsh days of the farmyard receded from the kitten's memory, only to be recalled at times by certain sights and smells – the rumble and stink of a tractor, cow dung on the hill tracks, hens squabbling and scratching.

The summer had been good that year and was followed by a mild, dry autumn. The weather did not harden till the first week of December. Frost came with the turn of the moon, on the night when the caravan family pulled out. At dusk they were seen through the uncurtained window eating their meal as usual and afterwards going about their accustomed tasks – washing up in a chipped enamel basin, emptying slops, shaking out bedding. Next morning they were gone, leaving behind them on the

trampled grass a straw mattress, a heap of empty tins and other rubbish, a debt of over two pounds for eggs and vegetables from Mr Trim – and the striped kitten.

Mrs Mostyn and Mrs Reece, emerging from the terrace of grey stone cottages which overlooked the pond for an after-breakfast chat over the wall, watched the kitten wandering and mewing over the campsite the other side of the pond.

'They seemed so fond of it,' Mrs Mostyn said, resting her large bosom on the coping. 'The little girl specially. Whatever come over them to go off like that and leave it?'

Mrs Reece detached her gaze from the distant view of her children ambling up the lane to meet the school bus at the crossroads.

'Too mean to feed it, I dare say, now it's half grown.'

'Can't be more'n four or five months.'

'Six, I'd guess.'

'Anyway, 'twouldn't eat much.'

'An extry mouth takes filling, even if 'tis only a cat's,' Mrs Reece stated with authority. 'And casual work's not easy come by in the winter.'

'Why don't he get a regular job then?'

'Goodness knows.'

The two women stared into the morning haze and pondered the mysterious ways of vagrants and the litter which stained the green of the campsite.

'Nice mess they've left for someone to clear up,' said Mrs Mostyn. 'Won't be me, that's certain.'

'An object lesson, that's what it is. Give 'em an inch they take a yard.'

'That's right.'

'And what's more, she took my best apron, or I'm a liar. Anyway it's not been seen since our line blew down. She swore she never, but I reckon that's where it went to all right.'

'Oh yes, I should reckon so. Can't keep their hands off anything, that kind can't. Ted's missing his hammer and he swears there's half a gallon of paraffin gone from the drum in our shed.'

'It were the apron our Jinny made for me in school, with the pansies on the border,' Mrs Reece was musing.

'The one she got the certificate for?'

'Ah, that's right.'

'What a shame!'

'Lovely, them pansies was. Every little stitch so neat and clean. Always been clever with her fingers, has our Jinny.'

But Mrs Mostyn's attention had strayed. Her gaze was fixed again on the abandoned kitten. Its unusual marking — black tabby rings on a dun ground, white nose and feet — made it conspicuous even from a distance.

' 'Tis a pretty little thing. I'd be tempted to take it in meself if it wasn't for the old dog. He'd never abide it, not at his age.' Her eyes swivelled inquiringly to Mrs Reece, but Mrs Reece vehemently shook her head.

'No use looking to me,' she said. 'There's no room in our house for pets, nor food neither.'

'It could make do on scraps.'

'Not in our house it couldn't. With four growing

kids and a man that eats enough for a horse we don't have no scraps. A cockroach 'ud starve to death in my kitchen. It's not as if there was rabbits, you see,' she added more kindly. 'Time was when a cat could live for a week off a snared rabbit. But them days is gone, more's the pity.'

'Ah, there's many as miss the conies. I used to like to watch 'em running races up and down the hill.'

'They do say as four rabbits eat as much grass as a sheep.'

'Yes, and they say "less rabbits more corn, more corn cheaper bread". And bread's bin going up reg'lar every year since the rabbits went. So I don't take much account of sayings.'

They fell silent, while the fiery rim of the sun began to penetrate the mist.

'Frost last night,' said Mrs Reece.

'Ah. And more to come, I shouldn't wonder.'

'Be nice though, when the sun gets through.'

Already the sky was stained pink over the hill. Mrs Mostyn tucked her chilly hands in the cuffs of her cardigan.

From a cranny in the wall close beside her a wren suddenly uttered a string of notes so piercing that they made her jump.

'Noisy little scallywag,' she said fondly as she went in doors to make up the fire. 'I'll fetch him a bit of jam tart. He's that fond of pastry you wouldn't believe.'

The kitten, still mewing in bewilderment, had now extended its search to the clump of alders overhanging the pond, in whose branches the caravan children had built a platform. From here they had fished for minnows with a wire sieve suspended on a string. The pond, nearly always muddy, was a catchment for the springs and runnels of the hills. It was also the receptacle of awkward objects unwanted by the cottage dwellers. In a wet season when the level was high such deposits were hidden. In a dry one such as the present they stuck out, lending an aspect of fantasy to the scene. Two old motor tyres next to a length of bent pipe simulated the looped coils and snaky head of a sea monster. In the rushes that fringed the farther side lay the rusty remains of a lawn mower, its handles presented like the tusks of a lurking elephant.

The kitten climbed up to the platform which, exposed in the bare branches, was seen to be composed of rotten planks so precariously lodged that only a miracle could have held them together long enough to save the children from a ducking. There was nothing left here to comfort the searcher, no relic of their presence but a jam jar and a shred of blue ribbon. After carefully sniffing it over, the kitten clambered down from the platform and made for the old straw mattress, now rimmed with frost, which smelled of the boys who had slept on it. Here it settled down, curled up in the middle with its chin on its paws, to await their return.

The sun rose into a pale pink sky, slowly dissolving the haze and giving an illusion of warmth.

Mr Trim came out of his front door and stood stretching and blinking. Looking into the sun he did not at first see the empty patch on the green. It was Mrs Trim who noticed it when she followed him out.

'Well, I'm blessed – they've took and gone, Dad!'

'Who you talkin' about?'

'*Them.*'

The campers were always referred to in this way, never being accorded the dignity of a name. It was to be assumed that they had one, but not even Mr Mostyn, who was Halsey's foreman, knew what it was. At the farm the father was known as Jack, though his wife called him Jerry. The two boys had for a time attended school in the village with the Reece children but were in a lower grade and could

neither read nor write. Jinny Reece had tried to find out their surname but it sounded like none she had ever heard of. She reported that it was 'furrin'.

'Well, dang me,' said Mr Trim. 'They must have snook off in the middle of the night. And me owed a bill as long as yer arm.' He sucked his lips over his gums, for he never put his teeth in till midday, and shook his fist at the spot where the caravan had stood. 'There's gratitude for yer. Patched their old kettle for 'em, I did, and mended their stove and never took a penny piece. And this is what they done to me.' Forgetting that he was wearing slippers he aimed a vicious kick at the stone doorstep, then yelped and cursed.

'No good takin' on, Dad,' said Mrs Trim placidly. 'If you ask me, we're well rid of that lot.' She leaned over the wall to rap on Mrs Mostyn's scullery window. 'They've gone, Agnes!'

'I seen that,' Mrs Mostyn shouted back through the geraniums.

'Dad and me never heard a sound.'

'No more did we. Looked out this morning and there they was, gone.'

'Dad's owed a bill for eggs and such. He's proper put out.'

'Don't wonder. Reckon he'll never see that back.' Mr Trim was still muttering imprecations in the background.

'Hurt his bunion kicking the doorstep,' explained

Mrs Trim. 'Never does you no good to let yer temper git the upper hand. I'm always telling him.'

Mrs Mostyn giggled. Then she said disgustedly, 'Who'd ever have thought as how they'd sneak off like that? Left their little cat be'ind, too.'

'Left what?'

'That little stripey cat they brought from the farm.'

Mrs Trim shaded her shortsighted eyes and peered out over the green. She could just make out a dark blob on the faded ticking of the mattress.

'That it?'

'Ah, that's it.'

'Well, there's a nasty thing to go and do.'

'Reckoned one of us would give it a home, I dare say.'

'Well, I won't,' Mrs Trim said firmly. 'Got two cats of me own and don't want another.'

'Amy Reece don't want it, neither. What's to become of the creature?'

'It'll run back to the farm, I shouldn't wonder.'

'Ah, maybe it will when it gits hungry. Best take no notice of it.'

Maggie Trim went back indoors to wash her father-in-law's Sunday shirt. She had married his son many years ago when she was a pretty red-haired girl of twenty, and had become a widow almost as soon as she became a wife. Peter Trim had been drowned in a rough sea on the third day of their

Cornish honeymoon. His photograph, in the policeman's uniform that suited him so well, stood in the middle of the mantelpiece between the china dogs, but she scarcely ever looked at it now.

She was right about the kitten. After a day and a night of fruitless search it seemed to realize it was in trouble. The tug of old associations pulled it in the direction of the farm. It went slowly and with reluctance, in case the caravan should reappear as unaccountably as it had vanished. Three times, after hovering a little way off, it ran back to be reassured. Finally it seemed to come to a decision. Mrs Reece,

from her parlour window, saw it trot away up the lane.

'Got that much sense then,' she said to herself. 'Farm cats live on short rations. But at least it'll have shelter.' She went next door and shouted through the window to Mrs Mostyn, 'It's gone up the road!'

'Best thing it could do,' Mrs Mostyn shouted back. 'Hope it'll stay there, poor little creature, now the weather's broke.'

'I was going to do a bit of baking today, seeing we're right out of cake,' said Mrs Reece. 'But I mislike the look of that sky. Reckon I'll do the washing instead.'

'Don't look too bad to me. I'll leave mine for a bit.'

'Last time you put it off you didn't get it dry for a week.'

'Ah well,' said Mrs Trim philosophically. 'Got to take a chance sometimes.'

The instinct which led the striped kitten back to the barn where it was born did not prepare it for a hostile reception. Its mother, the black-and-white cat with the crooked tail, had recently had a new litter of five, of which only one was still living. The ginger tom had killed two, rats had taken another, and a fourth, the feeblest, she had accidentally smothered. Now she had decided to move the sole survivor to a place of greater safety. After diligent search she had found an ideal spot in the tractor shed.

No foodstuffs were stored here so there was nothing to attract rats or mice, and as a result the shed was neglected by hunting cats. She chose her moment carefully, waiting till the morning pan of milk was put down outside the dairy and all the other cats were pressing round it. Then she stealthily emerged from the hay barn with a black-and-white miniature of herself dangling limply from her jaws. Slipping between the wall of the shed and the manure cart she whisked into the shed and dropped her burden in the farthest and darkest corner behind the oil drums. She was about to lie down and suckle it when she heard a mew from somewhere close by. She sprang up and ran to the doorway. Standing outside, looking hopefully at her, was a half-grown striped kitten which did not belong to the colony at the farm. She did not recognize it as her own. It was an intruder and a potential danger. She crouched, her

eyes narrowed and blazing, a ridge of hair rising along her spine.

The kitten had trotted into the yard a few minutes earlier. It had halted and stared around, recognizing the smells and shapes and sounds among which it had passed the first three months of its life. The heavy sweetish odour of the cows and the steaming tokens of their passage through the yard into the winter pasture beyond, the coughing grunt from the bull pen, rumble of men's voices from the milking shed, hiss and squirt of the hose, rattle and clank from the dairy and background whine of a radio – all was familiar to the small animal standing on the concrete and it reacted like a traveller to the sight of home after long absence.

None of the cats jostling round the milk pan in a tangle of tails and whiskers noticed the new arrival, nor did the she-cat creeping out of the barn towards the tractor shed with her burden. But the striped kitten saw *her*. It ran after her as far as the door of the shed and waited for her to reappear, announcing its presence by mewing.

The next moment it was knocked flat by a spitting

avalanche of teeth and claws. Stupefied by the suddenness of the attack and helpless under its mother's weight, the kitten could do no more than squirm and try to protect its throat. Tufts of fur flew about. The air was filled with yowls and screeches. The younger cats around the milk pan fled in alarm. The older ones ceased lapping and gave their attention to the spectacle. Over the bars of his pen rose the huge ringed muzzle of the Hereford bull. His dull eyes brightened, he blew out deep breaths and flicked his ears to and fro with interest.

'What the hell's going on?' Mr Halsey said to his dairyman.

'Just another cat fight,' Ted Mostyn said. Both men went to the door to watch. The event was not uncommon at the farm, but generally the fights were no more than skirmishes establishing territorial rights. Seldom were they so ferocious as this one.

'Surely that's the kitten Jack Kowalski took home for his kiddies?' said Mr Halsey suddenly.

'You're right,' said Ted. 'That's its mother on top of it. We'd best do summat or she'll kill it.'

He had been about to hose down the yard when the commotion started. He now switched the water full on and directed it at the combatants. The effect was immediate. The she-cat ran off. The kitten staggered to its feet and, crying in terror and bewilderment, fled through the gate and did not stop till it had covered a good half mile. By then it had lost all sense of direction and ran haphazardly over grass and ploughland, down lanes and footpaths, until it finally came to a halt in the churchyard on the outskirts of the village.

Here the bell was ringing for early service. At the gate stood four elderly women, huddling into their coats against the sharp wind. They were chatting within earshot of the kitten who crouched behind a tombstone, its heart racing and thumping after its flight.

One of the women had a high nasal voice rather like that of the caravan woman. For hours at a time the kitten had sat under the table listening to that

voice as it recounted the day's doings, scolded the children and exchanged banter with their father, and it pricked up its ears and peered eagerly round the tombstone. It chanced that the woman was wearing a coat edged with coarse dark fur. Mrs Kowalski had had a coat with dark fur on it. The coincidence was enough to make the kitten forget its fright and fill it with a wild hope. When the bell stopped ringing and the women entered the church it followed them in. The verger saw it, but not in time to prevent the intrusion. Now he didn't know whether to close the door or leave it open while he found the animal and chased it out. The rector was standing at the altar steps waiting for the door to be closed so that he could begin the service, so the verger decided to shut the door and make a discreet search.

In the event, search proved unnecessary. For the kitten came out of hiding and walked confidently up the aisle, stopping beside the pew containing the four women. The one nearest the aisle turned her head and gave a smothered shriek. The kitten was a deplorable sight. Blood trickled from a gash in its cheek and its coat was fouled with farmyard muck. The rector, confronted by this small apparition, was saved from having to take action by the verger who, with great presence of mind, crept up on tiptoe, scooped up the kitten in one big red hand and with the other opened the church door and tossed it out into the street. He assisted its departure with the toe

of his boot and then returned to sit piously in his usual seat, the one under the niche containing the statue of Saint Francis.

For the rest of that Sunday morning the kitten wandered about the village. Many people noticed it and were distressed by its woebegone appearance. A couple of weekend hikers, meeting it in the roadway, stopped to examine it more closely. They thought it must have been savaged by a dog.

'Poor little thing,' said the girl.

She offered it a slice of ham from her lunch pack.

The kitten sniffed with interest but did not take it. The drying blood had made its face so stiff that it could not eat.

'Well, it's not hungry anyway,' said the man, and

they walked on. The one danger to which the kitten had not been exposed that morning was attack from a dog. For the dogs that might have chased it were habitually kept on chains, and the furious barking they set up as soon as it came in sight was enough to keep it at a safe distance from them. While prowling round a council house dustbin it narrowly missed being hit by a stone flung at it by the owner, and twice it was nearly run over by car-borne churchgoers arriving for the mid-morning service. By the time the worshippers had come out again and were hastening home to their dinners the kitten had set off to find its way back to the campsite. Making a wide detour around Halsey's farm it got lost in a kale field, but by lucky chance found the rough track which Ted Mostyn used as a short cut in dry weather. Following the scent of the cowman's boots it finally arrived at the hamlet while the cottagers were sitting down to their meal.

Weary and in pain from the wound in its face it went to the pond to drink. There was an old broken wall round one end of the pond and on to this the kitten climbed. Here it crouched, its fur still damp from the drenching in the farmyard, trying to clean itself, and here it eventually curled up and slept.

During the afternoon Mrs Trim's two cats, a black and a grey who were brother and sister, came out of the cottage. In bad weather they generally went no farther than they had to, scratching a token hole in the flowerbed and skipping back indoors as quickly as they could.

The day being dry, they were in no hurry and strolled about, sniffing at crannies in the wall and interesting tracks in the grass.

From the day of its arrival they had resented the presence of the striped kitten in the hamlet. The

sister had plainly shown her feelings by hissing and bristling her fur whenever she caught sight of the interloper. But so long as it had the status of family pet and was in the company of the caravan children, the pair of them kept their distance. After its protectors mysteriously vanished they had watched its comings and goings with close attention. It was alone now and friendless. The time had come to re-assert their authority.

They could see the kitten sleeping on the wall and they picked their way over to it, crossing the green and avoiding the damp margins of the pond. Having jumped on to the wall, one on each side of their quarry, strategically poised for attack, they stared at it balefully, flattening their ears and lashing their tails. They were waiting for the kitten to waken and either accept the challenge or flee in disorder. It merely went on sleeping. They were unprepared for this passive counter-move and after a while they stopped glaring and tail-swishing. The grey female jumped down from the wall, stretched herself, yawned and walked away. The black cat, after licking a front paw with great energy, followed her. Neither of them gave the kitten another look.

# 2

THE cottagers did not know until next morning that the kitten had come back. Mrs Reece saw it when she opened her door to shake the mats – always her first job after her husband had gone bouncing and stuttering up the lane on his old motor-bike. The kitten was sitting on her step. Gave her quite a turn, she said later. She hastily shut the door. Once let a stray come in and you'd never be rid of it. Didn't do to feed it neither, come to that, if you didn't want to keep it. All the same, couldn't stand by and see it starve.

Three days now since them campers went, drat them, thought Mrs Reece fretfully. Why didn't they take their pet with them instead of turning it loose to pester other people? Just like the *diddakois*. After a few minutes of fuming indecision she filled a pie dish with bread and milk and went out by her back door. She went around the angle of the wall – her cottage was at the north end of the row of three – across the green to the pond and on to the flat ground beyond it. She called 'Puss, puss, puss!' and the striped kitten bounded out through the front gate and came flying after her.

Having deposited the pie dish at a point, she hoped, far enough from the cottages to be unidentified with any particular occupant, Mrs Reece stood back and watched the kitten eagerly lapping. She did not stroke it for fear of encouraging it. But she had noticed its gashed face, on which the blood had now congealed and blackened, and she shrewdly guessed the cause.

'Druv you away, did they? Well now, what's to be done with you? Us'll have to put our heads together and think of summat.'

Later that morning Mrs Reece, Mrs Mostyn and Mrs Trim gathered in Mrs Trim's kitchen over cocoa and ginger biscuits to discuss the matter. The hope at first held by the other two that Mrs Trim might be induced to offer the kitten a home had been short-lived.

'I can't afford to keep another, and that's flat,' she said with finality. 'Besides, there's Dad's feelings to be considered. He's bitter about the egg bill.' If the matter was put to Dad she knew exactly what he'd say. He'd say it was hard enough that he should be a couple of pound to the bad on account of them campers, let alone be asked to harbour their danged cat for 'em. 'And you couldn't blame him really.' Mrs Reece and Mrs Mostyn felt obliged to agree.

'I don't see it starving,' Mrs Trim went on. 'Not when there's mice and birds to be had. It'll go wild afore long, I shouldn't wonder.'

'Be kinder to put it away,' was Mrs Reece's opinion. 'Ted would do it,' she added, looking at Mrs Mostyn.

'I dare say he would. But I shan't ask him.'

'Nor I won't ask Dad neither,' said Mrs Trim, 'not till we've tried other ways. If you're so set on the notion, Amy, why not get Bert to do it?'

'Bert?' Mrs Reece exclaimed with derision. 'Not him! He's a proper softie, Bert is, for all his size. Won't so much as squash a beetle.'

'Ah, that's true,' said Mrs Trim. 'He don't like it when Dad shoots the rooks that pinch corn from the hen run.'

'He's a rare one, my Bert is. You don't often see a man as don't want to kill nothing. Well, you two can do what you like.'

'Well, I dunno, I'm sure.'

No solution was reached. The only point on which all three were agreed was the wickedness of the people responsible for the whole tiresome matter.

Just then a series of squeaks was heard outside. Three heads turned to watch a tall figure wheeling a bicycle down the rough path to the lane. There was the person best fitted to offer a home to the kitten, but to adopt a homeless animal was not a thing you could ask of someone with whom you were not on speaking terms.

'There she goes,' said Mrs Reece, dunking another biscuit in her cocoa. 'The old misery! Reckon she's got vinegar instead of blood in her veins.'

'I wonder why she ever wanted to come and live here.'

'That's what we'd all like to know.'

'And no one's likely to tell us, that's for sure. Least of all *her*.'

Of the two larger cottages in the hamlet, one was the holiday cottage of a solicitor named Ferguson and was used only during the summer months and for an occasional weekend in the winter. The other, so far as her neighbours were concerned, might not have been occupied at all, for it belonged to Miss Coker. Her gaunt figure in its raincoat and stout boots was a familiar sight, yet little more was known about her now than when she had first come to live there. She kept to herself, silent and solitary. It was thought that her odd behaviour hid some dark secret, but the truth was that this poor lady had no secret save the great sorrow that had changed her life.

She had once been a lively and attractive girl, one of an affectionate family living in a London suburb. Then one night the family house burned to the ground before anyone could be saved and at one blow Miss Coker lost everyone who was dear to her. She escaped only because she had gone out to look for their cat which had been missing all day. She never found the cat and she never forgave it for saving her life.

She lay in hospital for many months, ill with shock, and when at last she was able to leave she was a different person, irritable, morose, shunning human company. She left London to look for a dwelling place lonely enough to suit her. Eventually she found the cottage in the hamlet, and since she came to live there she never spoke to the other inhabitants except to complain. Mrs Mostyn's radio was too loud. The Reece children had thrown stones on to her roof. Mrs Trim's cats trespassed in her garden. This last infuriated her more than anything else, for her grievance against one particular cat had grown till it included all cats.

She first became aware of the kitten on the fifth day of its ordeal, towards the end of a grey and lowering afternoon. She had cycled back from the village and was pushing her machine up the track over the green when she saw a small animal sitting outside the Trims' front door. As she passed, the

door opened a few inches and Mr Trim's craggy red face appeared in the crack.

'Danged if it ain't still there!'

A missile of some sort – it looked like an old cloth cap – came hurtling out and narrowly missed its target. Then the door slammed with a noise like a thunderclap. But to Miss Coker's surprise the animal, which she now saw to be a small tabby cat with white feet, did not retreat but continued to sit there staring patiently at the closed door.

It was watched by other eyes besides Miss Coker's. From within the cottage, snugly curled on the window seat, Mrs Trim's two cats gazed calmly out at the intruder. They had become resigned to its presence in their domain. On the previous evening the female had even allowed the kitten to share the saucer of milk put out each night by Mr Trim. The milk was not intended for the cats but for his hedgehog. Unbeknown to him, however, the hedgehog had hibernated earlier than usual and the milk was stealthily consumed by other prowlers until he caught them at it.

Miss Coker saw the kitten again next morning from the window of her bedroom. It was prowling round the Fergusons' cottage, plainly seeking a way in. She made a mental note to keep her own doors and windows securely shut.

It had in fact already made several attempts to

get into the empty cottage. This time it unexpectedly succeeded.

Two of the ground floor windows had been opened by Mr Trim in the course of his caretaking duties. Once a week, whatever the weather, he aired the cottage for precisely two hours. In the summer he kept the garden tidy, mowing the front lawn, trimming the hedge and scything the long grass at the back.

Promptly at ten o'clock on this Friday morning he unlocked the front door, went into the living room and opened the windows and then went into the kitchen where he baited and set the mouse trap.

The kitten, watching from the rank grass under the apple trees, heard the casement hinges creak. As soon as the click of the garden gate signalled Mr Trim's departure it jumped on to the sill and into the living room of the cottage.

The air smelt stuffy and dank. No fire had been lit since September. The walls, to which layers of paper clung like snails on a stone, were stained with rising damp. The woodwork glistened with moisture.

The kitten crept about with extreme caution. This was the first time it had been inside a house. The vastness of it, the many objects and their strange smells, were alarming. After inspecting everything in the room very thoroughly and feeling reassured that there was no immediate danger, it gave its attention to the narrow boxed-in staircase rising from one corner to the upper floor. Sniffing at every tread and inhaling dust from the haircord carpet it was seized by a fit of sneezing. When this was over, it was about to make a daring scurry to the top of the stairs when a loud metallic *snap* sounded from somewhere down below. The kitten crouched flat in alarm. The noise was not repeated and nothing further happened, so after an interval it went to investigate. The sound had come from the kitchen, where the trap set by Mr Trim had found an early victim. The mouse was a young one, plump and sleek. It sprawled flat under the metal flange which had broken its back, tiny black eyes like beads of jet as yet unclouded, a spot of blood on its mouth. The kitten smelled the blood and was at once reminded of its hunger. It began to paw the mouse, tentatively at first, nervous of the trap, then more wildly as its hunger grew unbearable. It seized the mouse, lift-

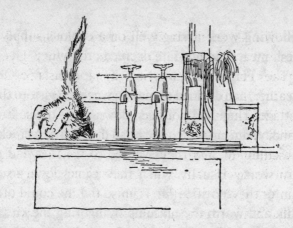

ing the trap as well, and carried it to a recess under the sink. Here, after frantic experiment, it discovered how to hold down the trap while eating the mouse. It also ate the piece of cheese impaled on the wire beside the spring. When nothing was left it washed its face and tried to scrub off the dried blood, but the effort was too painful. It leapt on to the draining board and drank some water from a puddle in the sink, then took a short nap, after which it returned to the living room, mounted the stairs and continued to explore the premises.

The whole place smelled of mice. The kitten was in one of the bedrooms investigating a hole in the skirting board when Mr Trim came back to shut up the cottage. He was in a hurry and did not go into the kitchen but simply closed the front windows and went straight out again, locking the door behind him and imprisoning the kitten for the rest of that day and night. It might well have stayed there all the following week, living well on a copious supply of fresh meat, had not fate decreed otherwise.

The Fergusons, worried by forecasts of bad weather, had decided to make a weekend visit to their cottage. They had not been down since the summer holiday, during which they had discovered a crack in the chimney, and they wanted to see if it had got any worse. Usually when they came down in the winter they notified Mr Trim so that he could order milk and warm the place up by lighting the kitchen stove. But this time the decision had been taken on the spur of the moment. Within an hour or two of forming the plan they were driving south over roads still slippery with frost.

They arrived, to the accompaniment of blasts of the horn, just as Mr Trim was sitting down to his favourite meal, a plate of fat bacon and cabbage greens.

'I'll keep it hot, Dad,' his daughter-in-law said soothingly as the old man rose, grumbling fiercely.

'You do that, girl, you do that.' Mr Trim smacked on his old cloth cap, took the key off the dresser and stumped out. Neither of the Fergusons apologized for arriving without warning. It was not their way. Mrs Ferguson was a tall blonde woman with a loud voice and sharp manner. Mr Ferguson was small, quiet and kindly. They were a happy couple and took a real interest in the countryside, especially in bird life. Their garden was a little sanctuary. In the

branches of the apple trees hung nest boxes, feeding tables, coconut shells and various containers for food. One of Mr Trim's duties was to keep the containers filled with peanuts, crushed corn, sunflower seeds and other delicacies, of which a plentiful supply was stored in the cottage and much appreciated by colonies of mice.

Barely had Mr Trim exchanged a word of greeting with Mr Ferguson, when he was assailed by Mrs Ferguson from the front garden.

'You've cut back the elder bushes. I've told you more than once never to cut elder. The berries provide essential food for the birds.'

Following her into the cottage he was further attacked when she saw a strip of peeling wallpaper.

'Look at that! I expect you to attend to matters

of this kind without being told. There's plenty of paste in the cupboard.'

Mr Trim's stomach was rumbling with emptiness and his feelings were hurt. He had made two attempts to stick down that strip of paper but the wall was too wet to hold it. Resisting the temptation to 'let fly' at her he pursed up his mouth, threw the door key down on the kitchen table and was in the act of making a dignified exit when the voice

sounded again, this time from upstairs. Mrs Ferguson had made a shocking discovery.

'There's a cat on my bed!' Had it been a deadly viper the words could not have expressed more horror. 'Whose is it, and what is it doing here?'

Mr Trim, halted in mid-flight on the doorstep, shouted back, 'What like of a cat?'

'Tabby-coloured. White feet.'

'Ain't nobody's. That's a stray, that is.'

Mrs Ferguson came downstairs shooing the kitten before her. Ears flat, very frightened, it shot out of the front door between Mr Trim's legs and vanished through a gap in the hedge.

'You know perfectly well I won't have stray cats about the place killing my birds. If a home can't be found for it, you must destroy it. The kindest thing you can do for a homeless cat is to kill it.'

'I don't see fer why. A cat's not like a dog. 'Twill fend for itself.'

'Precisely. And take every bird within range, especially half tame birds like these. You have a gun, I suppose?' Mr Trim nodded.

'Then use it.'

'I don't hold wi' shooting cats.'

Seeing the mutinous set of the old man's jaw, Mrs Ferguson used a softer tone. She knew her man, or thought she did.

'Now look here. There's a way of settling this to everyone's satisfaction. I'll give you a pound and your bus fare to catch that cat and take it into town to the RSPCA people who will put it painlessly to sleep.' Without waiting for a reply she thrust a note into his hand, gave him a gentle push and shut the door behind him.

Mr Trim went thoughtfully down the path, tucking the note into his trouser pocket. He did not mention the matter to his daughter-in-law while eating his belated dinner. This thing required proper thinking out. He devoted the best part of the afternoon to it while feeding syrup to his bees.

There were three choices. He could carry out the order and keep the money. He could keep the money and ignore the order. Or he could hand the money to Ted Mostyn in the certainty that Mrs Ferguson's wishes would be obeyed. Ted would quietly knock the little cat on the head and drown it. Born of generations of countrymen he was not squeamish in such matters. He knew that an animal living wild is often worse off than a tame one with a bad master. There is no master so harsh as nature.

It was Mostyn who did away with some of the endless litters of kittens at the farm. It was not because of any lack of confidence in him that Mr Trim decided not to delegate the task to Ted. Nor was it due to pity for the animal concerned, for the fact was that Mr Trim had no love for stray cats and would sooner have seen the kitten dead than alive. It was not even due to his natural reluctance to part with money. The reason that made him choose the second course was simply this: that although they had owned their cottage for a dozen years the Fergusons were still regarded as invaders. Foreigners, that's what they were, and Mr Trim wouldn't be put upon by the like of them, not he. What he was actually going to do could be summed up in a single word. Nothing.

The Fergusons did not linger at the cottage after assuring themselves that the condition of the chimney was no worse. They left the same afternoon for the comfort of their house in Bath. Mr Trim was hoeing his vegetable patch when they came to say good-bye and to return the key.

'Remember now,' Mrs Ferguson said, 'I'm counting on you.'

'More fool you then,' muttered Mr Trim as they drove off.

The kitten returned to the cottage at dusk that evening, tried all the windows, standing on its hind legs to paw at the glass, then sniffed under the front door. The smell of mice coming through the gap below the weatherboarding was mouth-watering. Eventually it gave up trying to get in and returned to the occupied cottages.

It was not yet noticeably thinner, for Mrs Reece filled the pie dish with bread and milk and her children added scraps which they saved from their school lunches.

Jinny said to her mother at supper on Sunday evening, 'Why can't we have the kitten, Mum?'

'Because I say so, that's why.'

It was not often that Amy Reece snapped at her elder daughter whom she dearly loved, but she had had a trying day. She had discovered she was going to have another baby and she did not want another.

The house was too crowded already and she had a job to manage on Bert's wages as it was, with food so dear. And half a pailful of soot had fallen down the kitchen chimney and made a dreadful mess that had taken hours to clean up. Not a minute all day had she been able to put her feet up. And now Jinny had started on again about that dratted cat. She couldn't have chosen a worse moment.

'It's only small, Mum. It won't eat much.'

'Won't always be small, will it? Talk sense. Costs a lot now to feed a cat. Them tinned foods are dear. Anyway, ten to one it isn't house trained. I've got enough to do without cleaning up cat mess.'

'I'll clean it up, Mum.'

'Will you *stop it*, Jinny? I've said *no* and there's an end of it.' Her flare of anger was extinguished when she saw the child's eyes misting with tears. It took a lot to make Jinny cry. 'There's nothing to stop you finding a home for it,' she said more gently. 'You could pass the word around at school. Like as not there'll be someone who knows someone as wants a cat.'

Jinny went out of the room without replying. But the idea had taken root in her mind. During recess on Monday morning she talked to Miss Johnson about the kitten.

Miss Johnson's character made her a certain ally. She had shocked the appointments board by declaring that it was as important to teach children to love animals as to teach them to read and write, and she had made some unheard-of innovations, not all of which were successful. She encouraged the children to keep unusual pets and to bring them into school. Jackdaws, leverets, a ferret, a white rat and a tame fox cub romped and rampaged through the classroom during nature hour – which naturally was the favourite hour of the week with the pupils but not with the school cleaners.

Now she sat listening attentively to Jinny Reece's plea, as she listened to all the problems her children brought her. When Jinny had finished she said, 'I should like to adopt it myself, but I can't.'

'Why can't you?'

'My landlady won't allow it. No pets. That's her rule.'

'Not even a budgie?' Jinny was shocked.

'Not even a budgie. Anyway I wouldn't want that. Birds were meant to fly about, not to be shut up in cages.'

'It'd learn to talk and be company for you.'

'I assure you I have to listen to enough silly chatter from human beings, let alone from parakeets.'

'Well, I think it's a daft rule.'

'No, it isn't daft. But even if it were, she has a right to make it. If I choose to live in her house I must keep her rules, just as you must keep mine when you're in school.'

'What can we do about the kitten, Miss Johnson? One of us got to do something or it'll die.'

'I'll think of something. Go into the playground now while I make some phone calls.'

After about twenty minutes Miss Johnson rapped on the window and beckoned Jinny in.

'I tried the pet shop, but they have enough kittens in stock. I tried the cats' home in Mulcaster. They have a case of flu and are refusing admissions. But I think I may have drawn lucky at the police station. The sergeant tells me that a white cat wearing a little

collar with a bell was picked up dead in the road last week, outside the supermarket.'

'That's Granny Oddams' cat!'

'Yes, sad to say. They identified it easily. Poor Granny must be grieving and she might be glad to have another cat. I shall go to see her this evening. I owe her a visit anyway.'

Jinny went blithely home that day and told her mother that everything was going to be all right now that Miss Johnson had taken the matter in hand.

True to her promise, the schoolmistress set out that evening for the cottage at the end of the lane opposite the post office. When she had last seen Granny Oddams the old lady was energetically gardening and feeling, as she said, fit as a spring chicken despite her eighty-odd years. But now the garden, once so neat, wore a neglected look. Curtains were drawn over the front windows. Granny had taken to her bed, her neighbours said.

Miss Johnson climbed up to the small stuffy bedroom. One look was enough to convince her that Granny Oddams would never get up again, that she had already forgotten her lost pet and would have no need of another. She stooped and kissed the dry sunken cheek, then she went away.

The kitten, meanwhile, had taken up its daily vigil outside the Mostyns' cottage. It was not seeking food so much as companionship, the friendly sounds and smells of human dwellings. Nor did it yet suffer from cold, for its coat was thick and it caught an occasional fieldmouse to supplement the food put out for it. There was a heavy frost each night, but with the old straw mattress for a bed the cold did not matter. So long as the rain held off the kitten fared reasonably well, but the fine spell was coming to an end. Mr Trim's barometer had been falling steadily for twenty-four hours and the elms along the lane had begun to tremble and creak. Starlings stayed close to their roosts. Whirling gusts whipped up the last of the leaves and flung them about. Fowls went early to bed. The cottage women fetched in coal and kindling, sensing the coming storm. Miss Coker made the rounds of her casement windows.

The striped kitten was restless, aware of the need to find shelter but reluctant to leave the campsite. The mattress and the rubbish strewn around it were the last relics of its haven. Also, from this point it could look across the green to the row of cottages and watch their windows light up at twilight. It stood now, in the rising wind, uncertain whether to go or stay. It had learned the futility of seeking shelter at the cottages. There was not a shed, out-house or privy whose door was left unlocked at

night. While the lighted windows shone out in the dusk it stayed, as fascinated as a child by a row of bright beads. But the pleasure was shortlived. When the darkness fell the curtains were drawn and it was only when a door opened to let someone in or out, or a curtain hung askew, that a yellow shaft broke the black dark.

It settled down in the lee of the broken stone wall – a wise choice, for the wind was blowing from the east and the wall gave what shelter was to be had. But during the night the wind veered to the north and increased in force. When dawn came the hills were blotted out behind a sullen grey blanket of rain and sleet. By the time full daylight came the ground was soaked and the kitten also. It got up but could scarcely stand against the wind. Half trotting, half blown along, it made its way over to the campsite to see if there was anything left to eat in the pie dish. The dish was no longer there, having been whirled into the pond along with the mattress and most of the rubbish. The kitten crouched on the spot where the pie dish had been and waited hour after hour for Mrs Reece to appear, until it was almost too stiff to move. Then it began to scratch forlornly among the half-buried tins on what remained of the rubbish heap and found one that held, miraculously, a crust of meat round the rim.

After this it wasted no more time but set out on a resolute search for shelter.

# 3

MRS REECE did not appear that day or the next because her husband had been taken ill. He had got up on Tuesday not feeling quite himself but insisting that he was fit enough to go to work. Before midday he was driven home from the quarry by Willie Cobb, one of his mates. Mrs Reece, peering through her rain-lashed window, saw the truck coming down the lane, guessed what had happened and went quickly into action.

First she sent her two younger children next door to be minded by Mrs Mostyn. Then she filled the kettles, banked up the stove, rushed upstairs for Bert's nightshirt and put it to warm in front of the fire. Presently Bert was helped indoors, green in the face and doubled up with pain, stripped of his wet clothes and put to bed. Willie drove off, promising to call at the farm and telephone the doctor. Soon after Willie left Bert had his first bout of sickness.

Mrs Reece suspected food poisoning. All the quarrymen took lunch packs and sometimes for the sake of variety they shared the contents around. She stooped over Bert, who was lying back exhausted, and asked, 'You been eating one of them meat pies again?' He gave a feeble nod.

'I thought as much, you silly juggins. I've told you to leave shop pies alone. *Last* time Albie Waters

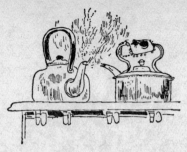

gave you one it made you sick. You know where he gets them from? From the railway caff, that's where, and glory knows how long they been lying around that dirty hole.'

'They never hurt Albie,' groaned Bert.

'Albie got a stomach like a garbage pail. You got a tetchy one, you know that. Ought to have more sense than eat such muck. Now look what you've gone and done,' she scolded as she wiped his pallid face. 'You gone and poisoned yourself. And serve you right.'

The scolding continued as she ran up and down with pans and towels, but the words were lost in the uproar of the storm. Window-panes rattled as if a giant were trying to break in. Hail drummed on the roof and the wind had the mad shriek of the norther.

Willie Cobb returned to say that the farm telephone was out of order, the line having been cut by a falling tree. He would have driven on into town to fetch the doctor but he couldn't get through. The road was blocked by the tree that had cut the line. Mrs Reece, however, was no longer worried for she knew now what was wrong with Bert.

'You go on back, Willie, I can manage. Bert will
be back at work in a couple of days, maybe a bit
more. I'll keep him at home till this weather lets up.'

Mrs Trim, popping in for the second time to offer
assistance, was blown halfway down the passage
before she could shut the door behind her.

'How is he?'

'Sorry for hisself. But he'll do.'

'What a day! Wonder you didn't keep Jinny and
Joey back from school.'

'I'd a mind to,' Mrs Reece said as she warmed another blanket. 'Just hark at that wind. I reckon it's
blowing a full gale.'

'I reckon so too.'

The two older children did not get home till after dusk. They had had to walk most of the way from school owing to the blocked road, and were drenched to the skin. By supper-time Joey was running a temperature, so he too was bundled off to bed. There were now two invalids in the Reeces' cottage. Jinny looked after her brother while Mrs Reece nursed Bert. Mrs Mostyn kept the two young ones with her. She enjoyed mothering them and tucking them into the big brass bed in the spare room.

During the night one of Mr Trim's hives was knocked over and some tiles were torn off his roof. Ted Mostyn came home after the early milking with a small tarpaulin and tried to help him tie it over the hole. But the task proved impossible in the teeth of the gale.

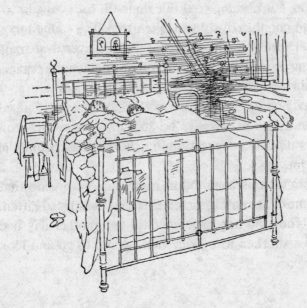

Neither the postman nor any of the tradesmen could get through to the hamlet, but Ted brought milk and bread for them all. He reported that the post office van had been sent to repair the telephone line, but nothing could be done till the council men had chopped away the fallen tree. The council men were doing the best they could with everybody nagging at them but they were fed up with the driving rain and the shrieking wind. There was a proper carry-on up on the main road, Ted said, and he hoped the milk lorry would be able to get through soon because they were running short of churns at the farm.

In all this commotion it was not surprising that none of the cottagers remembered the striped kitten.

They did not remember till yet another day had passed. Then Mrs Trim volunteered to go and look for it, taking with her some bits of fat bacon and other left-overs. The norther had not yet blown itself out. The elms still thrashed and groaned and the sleet was turning to snow. Mrs Trim could not see the kitten anywhere, so she put the scraps down in the usual place and hurried back to her warm kitchen.

Soon after she had gone the air above the campsite became alive with wingbeats and strident cries. Some gulls had seen the food and swooped down to snatch this unexpected bounty. But the Mostyns' dog Patch had also seen the pie dish being carried out and smelt the irresistible aroma trailing from it. He was a greedy dog and if there was one thing he loved more than another it was bacon fat. He ran across the green and tried to drive off the gulls, but they were too many for him, and unafraid. He snarled and snapped at the flailing wings, but in the end for all his efforts he got no more than a small morsel.

Mrs Mostyn also looked in vain for the kitten on her way up to the village. Snow was falling lightly and the air was raw, but it took more than this to stop Mrs Mostyn from making her weekly visit to her sister.

Miss Weekes, formerly the postmistress, lived in the tiny cottage next to the church hall. Every Thursday afternoon, the sisters met for tea and a gossip. Miss Weekes was lame and it took her a minute or two to hobble down the passage to the door. It was while Mrs Mostyn was waiting for the door to be opened that her eye was caught by the notice board hanging on the wall outside the hall. It was protected by a glass frame secured by a padlock. Miss Weekes, a prominent church worker and member of the parish council, kept the key. The only notice now displayed was an announcement of a jumble sale in aid of the vestry fund, three months out of date. The rest of the board was bare and this gave Mrs Mostyn the idea which was to cause one of the rare quarrels between her sister and herself.

While they were at tea she groped in her handbag for a pencil and a piece of paper, wrote out something and passed it across the table. Miss Weekes put down her rock cake, put on her glasses, took the slip of paper and read:

*Home wanted for nice little stray cat.*
*Apply next door.*

'What cat's this?' she asked.

'What it says. A stray. Been hanging round us near a fortnight. Some campers went and left it behind.'

'What's it like?'

'Little stripey cat with white feet.'

Miss Weekes screwed up her eyes reminiscently.

'There was a cat of that description in church last Sunday.'

'In church?'

'Yes. At early service. Must have followed us in. Came and sat in the middle of the aisle and gave us quite a turn. I think it had been fighting. Mr Timmins threw it out. I haven't seen it in the village since.'

'You wouldn't have. It's come back down our way.'

'Can't one of you take it in?'

'Nobody wants it.'

'Can't you get that daft woman, Miss What's-her-name, to adopt it? Do her good to have something to think about beside herself.'

'Of course it would, we all know that. But seeing she never says a word to anyone — not so much as pass the time of day — who's going to ask her?'

'Get Jinny Reece to do it. She's got a way with her.'

'Not with that old tartar she hasn't. It's out of the question. So will you put up the notice?'

'I can't.'

'Why not? You got the key.'

'The board is only for church notices, same as the one outside the school is for school notices. A thing like this doesn't belong anywhere.'

'Same as the cat, seemingly,' Mrs Mostyn said crossly.

'If you feel badly about it, then adopt it yourself.'

'You know I can't. The old dog's that jealous he'd have a fit.'

'Well, I can't help,' Miss Weekes said firmly.

'Meaning you won't. You never did like cats since poor old Tinker ate your blooming canary.'

'There's no need to rake up past history.'

'I will if I like,' Mrs Mostyn snapped. 'I don't see why you're so tetchy about your silly old notice board. Who's going to care if you do stick up a notice about a cat? It's a good cause, isn't it?'

'Rules are made to be kept.'

The affair ended with Mrs Mostyn banging down her teacup and marching out. After she had done so she was sorry and marched in again to apologize. Miss Weekes accepted the apology and gave her an affectionate kiss. But she still refused to put up the notice.

On her way home Mrs Mostyn reached the cross-road, where the lane branched off to the hamlet, at the same time as the school bus. She waited till Jinny and Joey Reece got off and all three walked down the lane together, holding their heads low

against the driving snow. The children's wind-stung faces looked like rosy apples. They clapped their hands, blew white jets of breath and jigged up and down. They were jubilant. It was the last day of term.

'Coo, isn't it cold!' cried Jinny. 'Miss Johnson says it'll be colder still when the wind drops. She told us to wear two pair of socks.'

'Miss Johnson got fur boots,' piped Joey.

'They aren't real fur,' he added hastily.

Miss Johnson had devoted the whole of one nature lesson to the trapping of wild animals for their fur. She told the children that most of the traps used were horribly cruel. She said that nobody who knew about these things would ever want to wear a fur coat. Afterwards some of the parents wrote to tell her the children had been upset by these disclosures. Miss

Johnson replied that she was glad to hear it, for this was what she intended.

'Coo, my ears are froze,' said Jinny.

To distract them Mrs Mostyn related how the striped kitten had gone to church on Sunday.

'Seemingly it's turned religious,' she said.

Joey yelped with laughter, but Jinny looked thoughtful.

'It used to be a custom for people to take their animals to church to be blessed, Miss Johnson told us.'

'Now it's been to church perhaps God will help it to find a home,' said Joey.

'I misdoubt it. God's apt to leave such things for us to deal with.'

'Why don't we then?'

'We're doing our best, love. We're all doing our best.'

'If we can't and Miss Johnson can't, then God'll have to,' Jinny said glumly. 'There's nobody else.'

The children scampered off, but despite the cold they did not go straight home. They went down to the pond to look for the kitten. There was no sign of it.

'I know it was there yesterday because I saw it,' said Jinny. 'It was settin' by the wall when we were going to school, and waiting for our Mum to come and feed it, only she didn't 'cos of our Dad. I wonder where it's gone now.'

'P'raps it's found a place to live,' said Joey. 'I wish it could come and live with us. Why won't our Mum let it come and live with us? Why can't we have the kitty for Christmas? I'm going to ask our Mum to give us the kitty for Christmas.'

'You won't get it.'

'Why?'

'Because she said not.'

'She feeds it, so why won't she let us keep it?'

'I expect she got her reasons,' Jinny said with a sigh. 'Grown-ups always got reasons.'

'Do you think it went back to the village and got run over, like Granny Oddams' cat?'

'How should I know? It might have. But somebody would have told us. Remember when Miss Mayberry's Ginger got hurt by that dog? We all heard about that soon's it happened.'

'He got well again, old Ginger did. And everybody knows him. Ain't many people know about the kitten. So who'd tell us?'

'I dunno, really,' said Jinny gloomily. 'Something could have happened to it. Be awful not to know. P'raps it's caught in a trap. That old man who lives in the bakery cottage, he sets traps for foxes.'

'Who said?'

'Mavis Bunting. She told me. She's his niece, or something. She says he catches a lot of foxes. He gets a pound for the skin. He got a badger once and sold it for shaving brushes. He's a horrible old man.'

'If he caught the kitten, would he sell its skin for a fur collar?'

'Don't talk like that.'

'Well, would he? He'd get as much as for a fox.

P'raps he has caught it and that's where it is, all dead and bloody, under a bush.'

Jinny was regretting having mentioned the old man. Joey had begun to sniffle and his voice was rising to a wail.

'It's dead, our kitty is, I know it's dead. It'll never come back. That old man killed it.'

'Stop it, Joey! Takin' on like that, all over nothing.'

'It's not nothing.' His grief was genuine and Jinny had to comfort him.

'The kitten isn't dead. It'll come back. There's all sorts of places where it could go to. Off in the woods somewhere. For all we know, someone might have found it and taken it in. Miss Johnson told a lot of people it was looking for a home and p'raps by now someone's offered. Don't be a baby. That's better. Haven't you got a hankie?'

'No.'

'Here's mine. Have a good blow.'

The kitten had not been seen because it had left the hamlet. It had gone to seek food and shelter in the spinney of birch and hazel down in the hollow below the rookery. The spinney was difficult to reach for the ground dropped steeply down from the lane, so the underbrush had not been cleared for many years and the place was a wild tangle harbouring a number of animals in relative safety. Here, in a fox earth they had appropriated from the owners, lived a family of badgers.

The last woodman to work in the spinney had built himself a hut of clapboard roofed with hazel branches and moss. It had served to store his tools and shelter him while he ate his lunch, but was a flimsy structure which should have collapsed long ago. As it was, the wind could not reach it and the denseness of the undergrowth held the rotten boards together. The woodman had made a pet of a grey squirrel that slept in his pocket while he cut and bound the split hazels that would be made into hurdles for sheep pens. The squirrel had its own entrance to the hut, a hole cut in the door about six inches wide. Both the woodman and his pet had been long dead but the hut had had a further occupant, a wild tom cat who lived there until, having escaped all attempts by local chicken keepers to kill him, he had died peacefully of old age. The hut still smelt of him and nothing but the urgent need for shelter would have driven the kitten to enter it. But the soft fur of a cat is a poor defence against the weather.

Wind pierces it; rain clings to it and chills the skin, making sleeping in the open a torment.

The kitten had been to the spinney before, hunting for woodmice, but had not discovered the hut until now. The hole in the door was just large enough for it to squeeze through, but it stopped halfway, its nose twitching in fear. After a long pause it felt sufficiently reassured to slip through all the way. The hut was certainly empty but it was far from weatherproof. Rain had poured through the dilapidated roof and left puddles on the earth floor, but at least the corners were dry, and offered a refuge from the frost and snow. The kitten was tempted to stay and sleep, but hunger drove it out again. It hunted for an hour without finding anything more satisfying than a few sluggish beetles among the dead leaves. The woodmice were safe in their holes under the tree roots. A few rabbits lived in the bramble thickets but did not emerge till nightfall when they went to graze in the pastures across the lane.

The tops of the birches were thrashing and moaning in the wind but down below in the underbrush all was so quiet that the sudden bark of a fox sounded the louder and more startling. The kitten froze in fear. This was the first time it had heard such a sound from near at hand. There had been foxes that prowled around the farm, but the dogs chased them off before they could get near the poultry yards. The kitten stayed very still, crouching behind a fallen birch log so nearly the same colour as itself as to make it almost invisible.

A fox trotted into view carrying a half-eaten wood pigeon. Within a few yards of the birch log it dropped the pigeon, lifted its head, barked again, and was answered by the scream of the vixen. She ran to join her mate and snatched up the remains of the pigeon. The sound of crunching bones reached the kitten and aggravated its hunger; but it did not dare to move till the foxes had gone. After a safe interval it crept out from behind the log and went to the spot where the foxes had been feeding. There among the feathers it found a small piece of flesh which it swallowed at a gulp. The tiny morsel only made it

more ravenous, but it feared to continue hunting while the foxes were near so it returned to the hut to wait till they had gone farther afield or back to their earth.

Unluckily they had done neither. The pigeon was all that the pair of them had eaten for two days and they were still too hungry to sleep. The vixen wandered back to lick up a few drops of blood among the feathers, and in doing so she picked up the trail of the kitten. The scent was one that was not unknown to her and which she now found faintly exciting. She followed it to the woodman's hut and peered in through the hole in the door. The hut had no window and was too dark inside for her to see the kitten; but the scent came strongly. She pushed her muzzle through the hole, sniffed and made a low eager sound in her throat. The kitten, suddenly confronted by the fierce mask with its gleaming eyes and teeth, backed into the farthest corner with the fur rising on its spine, petrified with terror.

After a moment or two the vixen, realizing that the hole was too small to admit more than her head, drew back and went away. But she only went as far as a clump of brambles a few yards down wind of the hut and settled there to wait till the kitten emerged again. She had to wait a long time till its heart ceased thumping and pangs of hunger forced it to take the risk. Even then, it took the greatest care, peeping through the doorway, sniffing the icy air

68

for any message of danger. Failing to pick up the scent of the vixen, it slipped silently through.

The vixen now saw her quarry for the first time. It was a slightly bigger animal than she had expected to see, and she hesitated before making her spring. That moment's uncertainty saved the kitten. It fled like the wind with the sharp muzzle and slashing jaws close behind; through the tangles of dogwood and elder, over brambles and deadwood, so fast that it seemed to be airborne. Instinct informed it that safety lay near human dwellings, so it made for the lane leading to the hamlet, clawing and scrambling up the steep bank, into the ditch and out again on to the iron-hard sandy surface.

It was the second night of the storm. Dusk had fallen early and Ted Mostyn was making his way home from the farm. Snow was driving into his face.

He kept his head tucked down into the collar of his
greatcoat and his eyes half closed, so he did not see
the kitten spring out of the spinney a few yards in
front of him, followed a moment later by its pur-
suer. But the vixen saw him and she quickly slipped
back into cover until the man had passed and then
padded away in the direction of the farm.

The kitten continued its headlong flight in the opposite direction, buffeted by the wind all the way.
Reaching Miss Coker's cottage it leapt on to the
garden wall and from there into a pear tree, unaware
that it was no longer pursued. In its exhausted state
it could not cling for long to the tossing branches and
was obliged to drop back on to the wall. From here it
could see, when a shaft of moonlight broke from the
storm-wracked sky, the open doorway of Miss
Coker's coal shed.

The door had been blown open and wrenched off its hinges by the gale and now lay flat on the worn flagstones of the yard. Scarcely believing this stroke of good fortune the kitten crept inside. Picking its way over the coal heap and between the wheels of Miss Coker's bicycle to the rearmost corner of the shed, it came upon an empty sack smelling of mice and old potatoes. On this it curled up for the rest of the night, thankful to escape at last from the torment of the wind and the wet.

When Miss Coker came to fill her coal scuttle next morning, she was dismayed and annoyed to find the door wrenched off, but as snow was now falling more heavily she did not stop to investigate. She scooped up some coal and hastened back indoors. She had not seen the kitten lying drowsing in the far corner, sleeping off the effects of its fright.

# 4

AWAKENED next day by intensified cold and hunger
the kitten crept out of the shed into a strange white
world. Snow lay everywhere as far as the eye could
see. The outlines of the frozen pond and the familiar
tracks across the green were quite lost. It was a different landscape. The kitten did not know what to
make of it at all. The very ground underfoot had
undergone some strange transformation. It was yield-
ing, treacherous, alarming. After a cautious ex-
amination that failed to solve the mystery the kitten
returned to the shed.

It had no food that day. Even if it had dared to
venture as far as the green the journey would have

been fruitless. The storm had driven a flock of gulls inland from the estuary and they circled incessantly over the hamlet waiting to swoop on the poultry yards at feeding time. Wheeling and crying, they rode the wind over the tossing trees, watching every movement below. When Mr Trim came from his back door with the chicken pail he had to fight them off, waving his arms and shouting threats. They were savage with hunger, for the ploughlands where they normally fed in rough weather were frozen hard. The sparrows that lived in the ivy were afraid to fly to the windowsill for breakfast crumbs. The raiders from the sea were there almost before the window closed. Having snatched the crumbs they beat their hard wings on the pane and stared into the room with pale cold eyes.

The kitten lay quietly watching the white flakes swirling in the space between the doorway of the shed and the back door of the cottage. It was still feeling the effects of its fright in the spinney and needed more sleep for full recovery. It was waiting for daylight to fade, for on the previous evening the kitten had made a marvellous discovery. Miss Coker's back door had a glass panel through which light shone into the yard from her kitchen, presenting to the occupant of the coal shed a glowing golden rectangle. The kitten lay basking happily in the delusion that heat as well as radiance came from it, stirring up memories of the lamplit caravan.

During the night the wind dropped and the sky cleared. The cottagers wakened to an ice-blue glittering morning, a grand day for a shopping excursion to the market town. The snow was crisp and firm underfoot. A little party set off soon after breakfast, the children in wool caps pulled over their ears, sliding and shouting and being scolded for making the path slippery.

Miss Coker heard them go by.

'Off to spend their money on rubbish,' she said with a sniff. She often spoke her thoughts aloud, though she tried to curb the habit. She was well aware that people who talked to themselves were supposed to be mad.

She needed to go to the village that morning to

74

buy batteries for her radio. Having put on her mackintosh and boots she went to the shed for her bicycle. It was then that she found the striped kitten. Angrily she shooed it out. It went a little way, then turned and looked at her and mewed. She shouted at it, 'Go away! Go on – away with you!'

So unusual was it for any sound to disturb the silence of Miss Coker's domain that Mr Reece, who was up and about but not yet well enough to go back to work, came over to see if the old girl was in trouble. When he saw the cause of the outburst he chuckled.

'So that's where it got to, the artful little cuss.'

'Who does this animal belong to?' Miss Coker demanded.

'Don't belong to nobody. Bin knockin' at all our doors, like, asking someone to take it in.'

'Well, *I* won't. And what's more, I won't have it hanging round here. I don't like cats. If I did, I'd have got one years ago.'

'No one's expecting you to feed it,' Mr Reece explained patiently. 'My missus'll go on doing that. She's not one to see an animal starve. But 'twouldn't

hurt you to let it sleep here while the cold's so bitter. They feel the cold, cats do, same as humans. Come the summer I dare say it'll run off to the woods.'

'It can run where it likes. I won't have it in my shed.'

Mr Reece pushed back his cap and gave her what he later described as 'a sarky look'. Then he shifted his gaze pointedly to the gaping doorway of the shed.

'Puzzle you to keep it out, seems to me.' He followed this up with a parting shaft as he walked off. 'I'd have offered to come and hang the door for yer, seeing it's only five days to Christmas and a time for folks to be neighbourly. But I misremembered. I've got other things to do.'

Miss Coker was left trembling with rage. She tried to prop the door in the entrance, but it was made of old ship's timbers and was so heavy that she could not lift more than one corner of it.

'Right old tartar she is,' Bert Reece said, recounting the episode to his family when they returned with their shopping at the end of the morning.

'Why don't she like cats? Did she say?' asked Jinny.

'No she didn't. I reckon she don't like nothing nor nobody. I reckon she's a bit batty. One day there'll be a van come to take her away to the 'sylum, you see if there ain't.'

'Can't come soon enough for me,' said Mrs Reece.

'Wouldn't it be good to have someone *nice* in that place, 'stead of an old misery as treats us all like dirt. There's few enough folks around here. Why did we have to get stuck with *her*?'

Joey was unwrapping the parcels.

'What's for dinner, Mum?'

'Sausages.'

'This ain't sausages.'

'No, that's a bit of summat special for yer Dad, to get his strength back so he can go to work. Been hanging about the house for long enough, he has, getting under my feet.' She had bought Bert a piece of rump steak.

'Mum —' Jinny said, smiling as she tipped the vegetables into the rack.

'Yes, love?'

'I've been thinking —'

'That's something!' said her father with a spurt of laughter.

'Don't joke, Dad. I've been thinking about Miss Coker. Miss Johnson says it's being lonely makes people act cranky, 'cos it's unnatural for humans. Humans are social animals.'

'I'm fed up with that Miss Johnson,' Bert bellowed. 'If that's what she's been telling yer she ought to know better. Animals is animals and people is people.'

'I was saying,' Jinny continued, 'that if somebody was to do something for that old lady, only nobody ever does –'

'Such as what, then?'

'Well, like fr'instance, if Dad was to hang the shed door for her. She might be different. She might talk to us sometimes.'

'Catch me putting myself out for the silly old faggot after the way she took on at me. Door can rot afore I'll hang it.'

'Yes, but, Dad –'

'That'll do now,' said Mrs Reece amiably. Her irritability had passed. One more in the family wouldn't make much difference. Be nice to have a baby in the house again.


Joey was giggling. After dinner, on the pretext of fetching a bucket of coal, he ran to Miss Coker's gate. From here he threw a clod of earth at her sitting room window and shouted, 'Silly old faggot, silly old faggot!' In the absence of any visible reaction

78

he repeated the phrase, jumping up and down and adding an invention of his own.

'Silly old faggot, face like a maggot!' Then he ran away as fast as he could.

The performance was wasted, for Miss Coker had not yet returned from the village. The exertion of pushing her bicycle all the way up the lane in such intense cold had brought on an attack of faintness. It came over her in the post office and she was obliged to ask for a chair to sit down on. Miss Mayberry, the postmistress, hurriedly brought a stool from behind the counter and helped her on to it.

'There, dearie – just put your head down atween your knees till I get the smelling bottle.'

The fumes of ammonia were so strong that Miss Coker's eyes watered and she could hardly get her breath. But almost at once she began to feel better and tried to get up. Miss Mayberry pushed her down again.

'You sit there and rest awhile, dearie, you won't be in my way. I'll be glad of company. You'd never credit it, but there's not been another soul come in all morning. It's this *Post Early for Christmas* appeal, you see. Everyone's bought their stamps and sent off their parcels days ago.'

She rattled on while Miss Coker itched to escape. But the difficulty was she could not produce any urgent reason to go. Her character and circumstances were too well known. Since she neither paid calls nor received them, had no friends and no occupation, she could hardly plead pressing business to attend to.

Miss Mayberry was one of the few people in the village who felt some sympathy for Miss Coker. A lonely woman herself, she knew what it was to need someone to talk to. What she could never have understood was that anyone would deliberately choose to live as Miss Coker did, neither seeking nor wanting companionship. Her mind running on these lines, she asked suddenly,

'Did you ever think of getting a dog? Or even a cat? A cat can be rare good company – and less trouble than a dog. Miss Weekes was telling me there's a little stray down your way that would be glad of a home.'

'I don't care for pet animals of any kind,' Miss Coker said.

'Ah well, that's a pity, that is. I wouldn't be without my old Ginger. But you know best what you want. And what you want this minute, by the look of you, is a drop of brandy. That'll put you right. It's a grand pick-me-up, a drop of brandy is. I'll run and get it.'

'Please don't trouble. I never touch it.'

Miss Coker made another attempt to get up off the stool and this time succeeded. Miss Mayberry still tried to detain her.

'How about a bar of chocolate then? Nourishing and sustaining. Helps to keep out the cold.'

'All right. I'll take a bar.'

'Plain or milk?'

'One of each.'

At last Miss Coker escaped. She quickly wheeled her bicycle away. But she was still not feeling very well and stopped outside the Stores to lean against the wall. This was unfortunate for she was then within earshot of the carpenter's yard and could hear the regular *swoosh-swoosh* of a plane. The sound stabbed through her with an almost physical pain, bringing back the image of her father. Mr Coker's hobby had been carpentry and woodwork. He had fitted up a little workshop in the cellar of their house and on most weekends was to be found, shirt-sleeved and ankle deep in shavings. The new smoothing plane had been her last birthday gift to him. He never wanted anything but tools and bits of wood.

Miss Coker closed her eyes and tried to blot out the memory. But it would not leave her. When she looked at the window display at the Stores she clearly saw, among the tins of soup and packets of cereal, her father's beaming face speckled with saw-dust. The faintness came over her again and she leaned heavily over her bicycle.

'Are you all right, miss?' asked the delivery boy, coming out at that moment with a carton of groceries.

'Yes, of course I am. Perfectly all right,' she snap-ped, adding sharply, 'You forgot my raisins last time. Can't you ever get the order right?'

'Sorry, miss.'

'Didn't you check it?'

'Yes, miss.'

'You couldn't have done. It's always the same. Always something forgotten.'

'Trust you to find something to moan about,' the boy muttered as he went off. 'Never miss a trick, you don't.'

Miss Coker rode home in a rage. She put her bi-cycle away in the shed, looking to see if the kitten was still there and noting with satisfaction that it was not.

It hadn't gone far this time, only as far as the ground in front of the cottages where it sat waiting hopefully for someone to appear with food. Eventually it was Mr Reece who, while his wife was busy washing up, brought out a basinful of meat scraps and bread soaked in gravy. He made a great show of putting down the basin where he could be certain Miss Coker would see him doing it. But he did not wait to see the food consumed. He had been sternly ordered not to stay out in the cold.

The kitten had eaten no more than a mouthful before it was set upon by the gulls, who had now been joined by a company of rooks and jackdaws. Buffeted on all sides, twice knocked off its feet and terrified by the savage pecks aimed at its eyes, the kitten ran off to its old retreat under the wall. Here it crouched and watched while the squawking quarrelling gang emptied the basin and flew off.

After wandering aimlessly about for the rest of the day it went back to the shed. Having been homeless for a fortnight it was content to have found at least a dry sleeping place.

The Reece children had seen the rooks and gulls attacking the kitten and would have run out to chase them away, but by the time they had changed their shoes and put on their coats and mufflers the birds had gone, leaving nothing but an empty basin.

'Are there any more scraps?' Jinny asked her mother.

'No, there aren't. Not till tomorrow.'

'The birds took it all, Mum.'

'They're hungry too.'

'The kitten's awful thin, Mum.'

'So are other creatures. 'Tis hungry weather.'

'Any bread, is there?'

'Not to spare, or you'll get none for your supper.'

'I don't mind.'

'Speak for yourself, child. The others will.'

'Mum, couldn't we, *please* –'

'*No.*'

Mrs Trim's two cats, from their vantage point between the flowerpots in the parlour window, had also watched the skirmish in front of the cottages. When it was over they yawned, jumped down, settled into an armchair on a pile of knitting and washed each other's ears.

The kitten, curled on the old potato sack, dozed away the afternoon. With twilight and darkness came something that compensated for hunger, loneliness and cold, a jewel that shone for it alone. Hour after hour, with its head resting peacefully on its paws, it gazed at Miss Coker's golden window.

It tried twice more to snatch a meal against vicious competition, and then gave up and did not leave the shed at all.

Miss Coker made it a rigid rule not to allow her mind to dwell on the past. It was a closed book, never to be opened. But having been reminded so sharply of her father that morning she could not stop thinking about him. And from him her thoughts wandered to other members of her family – to her mother, her dear mother, and her sister Lorna who was a school teacher and had just become engaged to a merchant navy officer. She even found herself thinking about the cat which had saved her life by running away before the fire. How extraordinary that it should have run off like that! Did it know what was going to happen? Had it had some mysterious warning? Cats were strange creatures. She remembered the day her sister brought it home from the local pet shop, just six weeks old and black as a coal. It was a time when they were going through some trouble, she couldn't recall exactly what.

'His name is Sooty,' Lorna said. 'He's going to bring us luck.'

And so he did, it seemed, for many years until – until the morning when her mother said 'Have you seen Sooty? He didn't come in last night. I'm a bit worried. He's never stayed out so long before.'

The day wore on and still he didn't appear. They all went into the garden and called and called. After tea Miss Coker went out to search the streets. Lorna said, 'I'd come with you, but I've got some papers to correct.'

She walked a long way, asking in the local shops if anyone had found a black cat or reported an injured one. And then there was the glow in the sky, and the fire engines, and everyone running – a gas explosion they said, in the basement. She jerked her mind back to the present, sat for a moment with her eyes closed and her hands tightly clenched; then rose and put on the kettle for her tea.

# 5

NEXT morning the Sunday peace of the hamlet was shattered by the arrival of Willie Cobb in the lorry. He brought with him Bert's motor bike which had been left at the quarry when he was taken ill, plus a long ladder and some scaffolding poles. The day had been set for a joint effort to mend the Trims' roof. Mrs Trim, after mopping up puddles for a week, had gone on strike.

Bert Reece had contributed a few tiles from his old ruined outhouse, lately re-roofed with corrugated iron. He and Willie pegged them while Ted Mostyn, at the top of the ladder, nailed new battens to the joists.

A lot of noise accompanied the work, shouts and bangs and men's laughter. Bert's laugh was the loudest, ringing throughout the hamlet in the still frosty air.

The sound of it infuriated Miss Coker who was still smarting from his impudent remarks about the cat. Moreover she had seen through his strategy. Plainly he had intended that frequent sight of the cat would finally break down her opposition. Thus it would find a home and the minds of those whose doors were barred to it would all feel easier. No doubt he thought, like so many others, that no one lived a solitary life from choice, and that by foisting

on to her a stray animal he would be doing both parties a kindness. Well, he thought wrong. She decided to go out for a walk to get away from the detestable sight and sound of him. She put on her thick boots and her warmest coat and set off up the lane. Work ceased for a moment and all heads turned to watch her go. She kept her own head resolutely averted and did not betray by the slightest movement that she was aware of their existence.

'That's good riddance,' chortled Bert when she was out of earshot. 'Like as not to put the evil eye on us, she is, and bring the whole bloomin' house down.'

'Think she's a witch then?' asked Willie.

'I dunno whether she is or not. But there was a time, not so long past, when folks would have said she was, and they'd have sewn her up in a sack and thrown her in the pond.'

The two older Reece children had been roped in

to help clean the tiles and knock out the old pegs.

'Is Miss Coker a witch?' Joey asked his sister.

'You heard what our dad said. I say she isn't. If she was one, she'd ride a broomstick 'stead of a bicycle.'

This struck Joey as enormously funny. He pranced about with a stick between his legs, hysterical with mirth.

When the work was done they all flocked into the cottage. Mr Trim had killed a couple of plump cockerels and Maggie Trim had roasted them with parsnips, potatoes and onions. She had set the table in the parlour for seven and a smaller one in the kitchen for the four junior members of the Reece family. She had made a huge apple pie for the adults and a bread pudding for the children.

Planned as a way for the Trims to thank their neighbours, the occasion became a real celebration when Amy Reece announced that she was going to have another baby. Maggie Trim brought out a gallon jar of her famous blackberry wine, and her

father-in-law produced from some secret hiding-place a bottle of whisky. There were whoops and whistles of amazement.

'Well, I'm blessed, Dad! Where have you been keeping that?' demanded Maggie.

'Never you mind.' Mr Trim pursed his lips and smirked as he poured out the carefully measured tots. 'Drink up and ask no questions. 'Tisn't often I buys it, but when I do it's good stuff, I promise you that.'

It was mid-afternoon before the meal was finished. Then the men were left to enjoy their pipes while the women washed up. Jinny scraped the plates.

'Can I have some scraps for the kitten, Mrs Mostyn?'

'Yes, love, you can take a few.'

'Now, Jinny,' said her mother, 'you know it's no use. The birds get it all. Anyway the kitten seems to have gone. Or maybe it's dead.'

'No, it's not, Mum. Dad saw it come out of Miss Coker's shed. He says it sleeps there. I could take it some food —'

'You'll do nothing of the kind. That old woman catches you on her place she wouldn't half kick up a rumpus. You keep away from there, do you hear? You don't want to get mixed up with *her*.'

'Yes, Mum, but —'

'Don't *pester*, Jinny. Keeps on and on about that dratted cat,' she said to Mrs Mostyn. 'I'll be glad when it's dead, and that's the truth, for I'm right sick of it.'

Mrs Mostyn said nothing. Her own opinion had altered lately and she now agreed with Amy Reece that the poor creature would be better off dead, but did not like to say so in front of Jinny. She decided privately to take up the matter with Ted and get some action.

When the party broke up and they had returned to their own cottage she sounded him out and found him amenable to the idea.

'Next time I see it around I'll try to catch it.'

'Ah, but it don't come around now. Stays in Miss Coker's shed, Bert says.'

'Well, I can't go in there after it, can I?'

'You could if you asked.'

'What, ask a favour of that old –'

'Not ask a favour. I mean, if you was to offer to do away with the cat, seeing as she hates it –'

'That'd be doing *her* a favour! No fear. Let her kill it herself if it bothers her so much.'

The subject was dropped from their conversation but not from Ted's mind. No one liked to think of an animal dying of slow starvation without a hand lifted to end its suffering. The trouble was, he could not take any action without approaching Miss Coker – unless he had a pretext for going into her shed without permission. Physically it was easy enough. He had only to scramble over the wall and walk in, now that the door was off. Take him less than a minute. Do it at night and ten to one she wouldn't see him or know anything about it. But if, by a flukey chance, she *did*, he would have to have a reason for being there; and for the life of him he couldn't think of one good enough. It was Patch who unexpectedly provided it.

The old spaniel was a surly dog, accustomed to getting his own way. He had brooded over his defeat by a flock of birds on Thursday and watched them daily as they circled over the green, growling at them, nursing his grudge.

He was watching them now from the parlour window while his owners sat by the fire and chatted over their tea.

Observing the way the birds' heads suddenly swivelled and their flight paths dropped lower he knew that they had spotted someone approaching with food. It was Joey Reece who came trudging past the Mostyns' window carrying a left-over slice of bread pudding, his pink face framed in a bala-clava, his boots crunching the hard-packed snow. Joey had discovered that if you threw a piece of bread, or suet crust, into the air the gulls would dive and catch it before it touched the ground. He was fascinated by the speed and beauty of the dive and the sun-dazzle on their wings as they soared up again. The rooks were not so clever as the gulls. They only got the few bits that fell uncaught and then had to fight to keep them.

Patch's eyes followed Joey down to the green, watching with intense interest till the food had been consumed and Joey, blowing on his frozen fingers, had run back home. Then he went to the door and whined to be let out.

Several of the rooks were strutting about searching for crumbs and did not notice Patch till he had stolen close. Then one of them turned and saw him. It sprang into the air with a squawk and Patch leapt after it. Somewhat to his surprise he caught it, sinking his teeth into the muscle of one of its wings. It threshed and screamed, twisted its head round and pecked his face, but he held on, making full use of his powerful jaws and heavy body. Having caught the bird he didn't know really what to do next. He

couldn't finish it off without letting go of it, and its sharp beak was jabbing painfully at his nose. He began to drag it aimlessly in the direction of the cottages. By this time dusk was falling and curtains were being drawn over the lighted windows. While Mrs Mostyn was drawing hers she caught sight of her dog going by carrying something black and struggling, which squawked like a fowl.

'Come here, Ted, quick. There goes our Patch. Whatever's that he's got in his mouth?'

Ted peered out. As he did so Patch disappeared round the end of the building.

'I didn't get sight of it for long enough to be certain,' Ted said, 'but it looked uncommon like Maggie Trim's little black bantam cock.'

'I thought so too. 'Twouldn't be the first time he's caught it, the old rascal. And I can't say I blame him. It taunts him something dreadful.'

'She should clip its wings so it can't get out of the run.'

'That's what I'm always telling her.'

'I'd better go after him,' Ted said. 'Be too bad if he killed it, today of all days.'

'Certainly would – specially as he growled at her this morning. His temper's getting worse and worse.'

Without waiting to put on his greatcoat Ted dashed out. He could hardly see the dog, the light was going so fast. But the dark parts of its coat showed up sufficiently against the snow to enable him to follow. He saw with consternation that Patch was making for Miss Coker's garden gate.

The dog squeezed under it and Ted vaulted over in hot pursuit. A pathway led from the front garden to the yard at the back of Miss Coker's cottage and it was somewhere along here that Patch dropped his burden. The bird flapped and scrambled away, and Ted to his relief recognized it for what it was. He called Patch to him with a low whistle and lifted him over the wall. He was about to climb after him when he remembered the conversation he had been having with his wife only ten minutes earlier. Here he was, standing right outside the coal shed. He stooped and looked in. There was just enough light coming through the doorway to reveal a small dark shape lying on a sack at the rear. It was alive, he could tell by the gleam of the eyes. The chance he was offered seemed so miraculously opportune that he could hardly refuse it.

He walked in, bending his head under the low beams, and made his way past the bicycle and other

objects till he was standing over the kitten. It made no move to get away from him but raised its head and looked into his face. He reached down, then drew back his hand. Why was he hesitating? It was such a scrap of a thing. One quick blow behind the head with the heel of his hand and it would be finished with, and no one the wiser.

The trouble was that with those eyes looking at him he simply couldn't do it. The kittens he had made away with at the farm had been so newly born that they were barely alive. Their unopened eyes saved them from recognizing the threat he represented. This one knew. He had no doubt of that. And because he couldn't face that recognition he backed away out of the shed.

'You gurt fool,' he muttered to himself as he scaled the wall and walked back to his cottage with his dog beside him. 'You mushy-hearted fool! You're as bad as Bert.'

That same evening Miss Coker discovered that the kitten had returned to her shed. She made no further attempt to drive it away, but this did not mean that her resistance had lessened. On the contrary, it had hardened, as a result of Bert Reece's impudence.

During the next two days she made a determined effort to forget the whole tiresome matter, and was both annoyed and perplexed to find that she could not do so. At frequent intervals while she sat by the fire, her slippered foot on the hearth, the image of the striped kitten came between her and the book on her lap. She saw it, as she had seen it for the last three mornings, lying on the sack at the back of the shed, quietly waiting. Waiting for what? For death?

Again she tried to thrust it from her mind. After all, she had been told that it was getting food, and now it had shelter as well. Many a stray was worse off. All the same, there was a disturbing factor somewhere. She couldn't identify it but neither could she be rid of it. It was with her now, niggling like a toothache. Something to do with – oh, whatever was it? Well, no matter. It couldn't be of any importance. She switched on her radio for the six o'clock news.

'*In many parts of the country fresh snow has fallen,*' said the bland voice of the announcer. '*Road and rail services are not yet affected and with only one more shopping day to Christmas the traffic has been heavier than –*'

Miss Coker switched off. But her hand stayed on the knob, halted there by a thought that had suddenly come to her. In this district there had been a further slight fall of snow forty-eight hours ago, but none since. The nagging unease at the back of her mind had some connection with this. Knowing that she would not be able to enjoy her book until she

had made a last effort to get rid of the aggravation she picked up a torch and went out through the kitchen door into the yard.

After the warmth of her living room the air was so biting that it hurt the lungs. Freezing again, she thought, as she crossed the few yards to the doorway of the shed. Holding the torch high she peered into the interior. The animal was still there. It lay facing the entrance, the wide open eyes glowing like emeralds. Miss Coker withdrew, frowning. Swinging the torch in a wide arc she studied the walled yard. Its white carpet was unsullied from corner to corner except for her own heavy prints and the tiny arrow tracks of birds. And at last she knew what it was that worried her. It was the absence of paw prints. If the cat had gone out to eat the food provided for it during the past two days there would be a double set of tracks between the coal shed and the garden wall. There weren't any. So it had not gone out.

Perhaps it wasn't hungry. But how could it not be hungry? There were no mice in the shed to her knowledge. Formerly there were scores of them. They used to eat her carrots and potatoes and even the daffodil bulbs. But now she no longer stored anything edible in the shed, so the mice had departed.

She was puzzled about the cat. It looked very thin. It might be ill, of course. In which case, in such bitter cold, it would probably not live much longer. Best to leave it alone and hope that death would come quickly.

Returning to her living room she banked up the fire and warmed her numbed feet. She picked up her book, but the words that she was reading made no sense. She began to smoulder with annoyance, both at herself for being so stupid, and at the wretched creature that disturbed her peace and would not be rejected. Why doesn't someone drive it away, she fumed. It's a conspiracy. They're all in it, trying to make me take it in. Why does it lie there, watching and waiting? I won't give in. Why should I? I won't. *I won't*.

She held out for one more night and one more day.

During the night she dreamed that she was taking a tea tray down to her father's workshop in the basement. He was making an enormous piece of furniture. It looked like a kind of wardrobe, except that it had a door made of iron. The dream started off as a funny one but it ended in a way that was frightening. For some reason they got into the wardrobe to have their tea, and then the iron door slammed and they couldn't get out. They banged and shouted, but nobody came, and then the wardrobe, which had been so huge, began to shrink. It became smaller and smaller till they were crushed together and could hardly breathe, and still no one came to the rescue.

'*Help! Help!*' they screamed.

The cries that Miss Coker uttered in her sleep, like those of a child in pain, were clearly audible to the kitten. In that icy stillness every sound was magnified. A snapping twig was like a gunshot. Even the rustle of roosting sparrows in the ivy outside the shed reached the animal within. So did the patter of claws as a big buck rat ran across the roof.

The rat was one of a foraging party travelling inland like the gulls from the frozen margins of the estuary.

While probing the ivy that covered the stone-built shed it came upon a hole in the roof. The storm that had damaged Mr Trim's cottage had dislodged a tile on the roof of the shed. Owing to the thickness of the ivy this had gone unnoticed.

The rat slipped neatly through the opening on to the beam spanning the structure. It sat for a moment, nose questing, eyes darting from side to side in the moon-broken dark. Soon it saw the animal lying motionless on the potato sack. The kitten's eyes were closed and its body temperature was so low that it gave out no scent. Concluding that it was dead, the rat ran a little way along the beam and was about to jump down and fulfil its natural function of scavenger when the kitten stirred and opened its eyes. The rat paused and squatted. From this point it had a better view of the animal below, which was more than twice as big as itself and not dead but alive. This called for different tactics. It withdrew to fetch the other members of the band, two females and a young one, which were waiting outside. In a few moments all four of them were ranged along the beam, hairless tails twitching, eyes burning like tiny red coals in the half-dark. The buck rat was grinding its long yellow teeth. Normally this sound would have recalled to the kitten one of the worst

terrors of its babyhood. But now it seemed unafraid and lay watching the rats with steadfast calm.

The big one moved forward an inch or so at a
time and the others closed up behind. They were
now directly above and the kitten could smell their
breath. Suddenly came a sound from outside. *Yik-
yik-yik, yik-yik-yik.*

Up the outer wall, over the roof and through the
hole, came a pair of stoats which had picked up the
trail of the rats. Expert little hunters, they wasted
no time and no effort. The rats bunched up together
and faced round. The stoats leapt straight at them,
gripping one of the females by the throat. The buck
rat came to her defence but in the constricted space
the fight became a scrimmage in which the dog
stoat was knocked off the beam. It was up again in
a flash, but its smaller mate was unable to hold the
female rat which broke away followed by the rest,
and they all went streaming out, pursuers and pursued, the squeaking and yikkering fading with distance till the silence of the winter night closed in
again. Throughout the skirmish the kitten made no

move. Now it dropped its head on its paws and lay as before, staring through the open doorway.

The moon waned and just before dawn a line of swans flew past. *Honka-honk!* they sang, high in the paling sky.

A barn owl floated out from the elms along the lane, silent as a puff of smoke drifting from shadow to shadow.

Another day dawned.

The Reece children spent that afternoon in Mr Trim's woodshed chopping sticks for his fire. It was not a labour of love but a penance.

Jinny was a persistent child who did not readily yield to opposition. She had cried herself to sleep after the party because her mother had said she wished the striped kitten was dead. When she wakened the next morning she was more determined than ever that it shouldn't die for lack of anything she herself could do to save it.

She said to Joey, 'There's only us, so we got to do it.'

'Do what then?'

'Feed the kitten in Miss Coker's shed.'

'How we going to get the food? Our Mum won't give us nothin'.'

'I'll show you.'

Jinny's plan was simple. Unfortunately it miscarried. At the first attempt, the pair of them had been caught redhanded filching scraps from the Trims' chicken pail, and this job was their reward.

'Ain't we done enough yet?' Joey wailed. 'I'm cold. I want my tea.'

'You heard what he said. We got to fill the box.'

It was a huge box and by four o'clock when the light was failing they were still at it. Mrs Trim brought them mugs of hot milk.

'If it was me I'd let you off,' she said. 'But Dad gits so mad. And it's not as if you done the little cat any good. Them pesky gulls take all you put out.'

'We wasn't going to put it out,' Jinny said. 'We was going to take it to Miss Coker's shed where the kitten sleeps.'

'God bless me, don't you go trespassin' there. You'll get into worse trouble.'

After Mrs Trim had gone back indoors Jinny burst out crossly, 'It's *her* fault. That old Miss Coker. Why don't she feed the kitten? Why don't she take it in? Why does she have to be so mean?'

This set Joey off giggling and he told how he had thrown earth at her window and called her a rude name. He expected Jinny's approval but did not get it. Instead, for no reason that she could have explained, she smacked him. He howled.

'What you go and do that for? I paid her out, didn't I?'

'You did a bad thing.'

The quarrel developed, reached a climax and suddenly fizzled out in the way their disputes generally did. By the time the box was full they were friends again and their mother was calling them in to tea. As it was Christmas Eve she gave them two things they specially loved, currant buns from the bakery and chocolate cake of her own making.

'Not that you deserve it,' she said, 'upsetting Mr Trim again. He's cut me short on the eggs this time.'

'Fine pair you are,' their father said.

'We made up for it, Dad,' said Jinny. 'I'm that tired I could drop.'

'Oh, are you? That's a pity. I thought as how you might start on a box-full for *me*. And there's Ted, too. He could do with some. We can keep you busy for days yet.' He chortled and cut himself another slice of cake. 'Got yer stocking ready to hang up for Santa Claus? Reckon he'll bring yer a nice little chopper all of yer very own.'

'Don't tease her, Bert,' said Amy Reece, but Jinny was not nettled as she sometimes was by her father's teasing. A picture had swum into her mind of a wood chopper among the oranges and nuts and boiled sweets and little wrapped presents in her Christmas stocking, and it was so funny that she began to laugh. Soon they were all laughing and the cosy kitchen was filled with fun and happiness.

After tea Jinny helped her mother put the two younger children to bed. Then she rejoined Joey for the remaining time before they too would be sent to bed. They played a game of snakes and ladders on the table in the parlour window, while Bert dozed over the local paper.

'Come on, it's your turn to throw,' said Joey impatiently. 'What you waiting for?'

Jinny had become inattentive.

'I was thinking about them carols Miss Johnson taught us.' The Reece children had been among

those selected to sing at the end-of-term concert. 'Seems a shame we only had a chance to sing 'em once. Think you can remember that one about the kings?'

'Course I can. I can remember 'em all. Or most.'

Jinny bent over the table to whisper. Joey's face at first registered protest, then reluctant acquiescence. They both got up and went into the hallway to put on coats, woollen caps, gloves and mufflers. Then they went out, closing the front door behind them unusually quietly.


Shortly before supper time Miss Coker suddenly rose from her chair, took the torch and went out to the shed.

As she approached the kitten stirred and raised its head. She stooped and passed her hand over its body.

She had to force herself to do it. This was the first time in more than thirty years that she had fondled a living creature. The touch of the soft fur caused something to happen inside her, some easing of the frozen heart. The kitten struggled to its feet, arching itself under her hand. The white parts of its coat were soiled with coal dust. She understood then that it was too weak to clean itself, let alone go in search of food.

She straightened up, stood for a moment fighting the inclination, walked off and stopped halfway across the yard. She looked back and saw that the kitten had followed her.

It crouched in the snow a few steps away, the tail dragging, eyes unnaturally big in the starved face. It stole forward a trifle. A few more tottering steps took it to Miss Coker's feet where it halted, uncertain, hovering between hope and fear.

She bent and picked it up. It lay passive in her arms, its bony little head pressed against her chin. Light as a bird it seemed. The draggled fur under her hand was not only without warmth but without resilience, more like the coat of a dead creature than a live one. The feeble heartbeats of the small body emphasized the strength of her own. Standing there alone in the ice-bound hush of the winter night she was suddenly and deeply aware of being *alive*. She saw, as if for the first time, the brilliance of the stars, the glittering beauty of the snow.

At this same moment she heard a burst of childish voices close at hand.

*'We three kings of Orien-tar!'*

The unsteady altos soared and dipped. Behind them, faint but sweet, sounded a far-off chime of church bells.

Miss Coker waited a minute or two, listening intently, before re-entering her cottage. She closed the kitchen door and took from the peg behind it an old knitted shawl she used when she went to fill her coal scuttle or empty the rubbish bucket. Next she pulled from under the sink a square shallow box which had once held apples. Lining the box with the shawl she set it down near the stove and laid the kitten in it while she warmed some milk. She filled a saucer and held the kitten in her arms while it lapped.

In her meat safe was a slice of liver she had bought for her supper. She cut off a portion and chopped it small, listening all the time to the carol singers outside her gate, who had now switched to *The Holly and the Ivy*. She fed the raw liver to the kitten, a tiny piece at a time, with long waits in between. Before it was finished the singers stopped. They had forgotten the second verse.

Miss Coker stood up and took from the dresser the two bars of chocolate she had bought at the post office store. She picked up the kitten and carried it down the hall to her front door, opened the door and stood on the step, beckoning to the children. Very cold, they were just on the point of going home. They stared at her, round-eyed with amazement. She beckoned again and held out the chocolate bars. Slowly, unbelievingly, they came up the path to take them. Neither child said anything. Nor did she.

They raced off with their news, bursting in and nearly knocking over the table on which Bert was trying to mend his old radio, both talking at once.

'Mum, Mum, she's got the kitten! She had it in her arms when she give us the choc!'

'She got it, Mum –'

'It had milk on its whiskers!'

'Well, dang me,' said Bert. 'Wonders never cease. Thing is, will she keep it?'

'I'd say she will,' Amy Reece said. 'Hard to turn it out again once you take in a stray.'

'She's bound to keep it, Mum. She were *stroking* it!' Their mother beamed fondly on the rosy sparkling faces.

'Well, thank goodness for that. Now we can all have a happy Christmas. Off with you to bed.'